JASPER & SCRUFF

TAKE A BOW

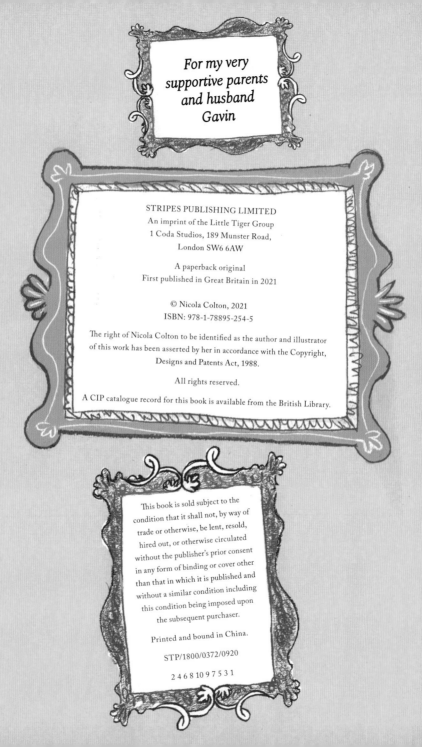

*For my very
supportive parents
and husband
Gavin*

STRIPES PUBLISHING LIMITED
An imprint of the Little Tiger Group
1 Coda Studios, 189 Munster Road,
London SW6 6AW

A paperback original
First published in Great Britain in 2021

© Nicola Colton, 2021
ISBN: 978-1-78895-254-5

The right of Nicola Colton to be identified as the author and illustrator
of this work has been asserted by her in accordance with the Copyright,
Designs and Patents Act, 1988.

All rights reserved.

A CIP catalogue record for this book is available from the British Library.

Printed and bound in China.

STP/1800/0372/0920

2 4 6 8 10 9 7 5 3 1

Nicola Colton

JASPER
& SCRUFF

TAKE A BOW

LITTLE TIGER

LONDON

J asper was the type of cat who liked to look his best. So every Tuesday, he had his whiskers waxed at Ruby's salon.

Scruff was the type of puppy who
liked chasing his ball through the mud.
So he was always getting mucky!

One day, Jasper persuaded his best
friend to come with him for a shampoo.

Scruff squirmed in his seat as Ruby
lathered his fur. But Ruby knew the
perfect way to calm a fidgety puppy.

"Scrub, scrubby-do.
I love a good shampoo..." she sang.

Scruff stopped wriggling and wagged
his tail in time to the rhythm.

"Wow, Ruby, you can carry a tune," said Jasper, admiring his newly waxed whiskers in the mirror. "Could you sing one of Alvis Pawsley's hits?"

"You're an Alvis fan?" asked Ruby. "Did you know that he's judging a talent show tomorrow?" She handed Jasper a flyer from a pile by the till.

Jasper remembered when he'd performed at the Velvet Theatre, back in his acting days.

"Can we enter?" yapped Scruff.
"I've already got an idea for our act..."

"Hmm," said Jasper.
"Are you going to audition, Ruby?"

"Who, me?" replied Ruby, blushing.
"I'm much too shy to sing on stage."

"Come on, Jasper!" Scruff jumped up,
sending a cloud of suds into the air.
"We'd better get a move on!"

Jasper hurried home after Scruff.
As they took a shortcut through
the park...

Splash!

Scruff dashed through a muddy puddle
and dived behind a bush. Dirt flew
every which way as he started to dig.

"Yuck!" said Jasper, shielding his face
with his paws. "You're filthy again, Scruff!"

"Yes!" yipped Scruff. "It's still here!"

His back legs wriggled in the air
as he disappeared inside the hole.

With a big heave, the puppy yanked
an old wooden box out of the ground.
He nudged off the lid with his nose
and jumped inside.

"Just watch this space and you will see ...
a transformation on the count of three!"
Scruff pulled the lid back on.

"One, two, three...

Hey Presto!"

Scruff sprang out of the box in
a plume of magic dust. He spun
round and tipped the top hat
that had appeared on his head.
"I am Scruff the Sensational!"

"Ack!" said Jasper, spluttering out
sparkles. "Can we stop mucking about and
get home? I need to practise *my* act."

"Oh," said Scruff, his tail drooping.
"I thought we could do a magic act
together. I even have a spare wand."

"Sorry, Scruff, but I've got
something else in mind," said Jasper.
"May the best cat win!"

The next afternoon a queue ran
all the way around the block from
Snootington Town Hall. It seemed
like the whole town had turned
up to audition!

Jasper and Scruff joined the back
of the line behind an alpaca on
a unicycle.

"I'm Audrey," she bleated. "Ooh, are you two doing a magic act?"

"Well, *he* is," said Jasper. "My act is somewhat more refined."

The town clock struck three. A wave of nervous whispering swept over the queue as a gazelle holding a clipboard came to fetch the first contestant.

"It's Salty Cyril!" said Scruff, as their friend stepped through the door.

Less than a minute later Cyril was back,
his tail between his legs.

"Ahoy!" said Cyril, spotting his friends.
"I was halfway through 'Yo Ho Ho and a
Scoop o' Ice Cream' when I dropped
me drum. Marvello told me to stick
to servin' ice cream."

"That was a bit mean," said Scruff, as Cyril shuffled away.

"It is a talent show," said Jasper. "Only the best will do!"

The pair were almost at the front of the queue when they heard a commotion behind them.

Before they knew it, Lady Catterly had pushed her way past. Reginald and Oswald followed.

"What are the Sophisticats doing here?"
asked Scruff.

"No idea," groaned Jasper.

Audrey was practising her routine one
last time. As she completed a triple-
twist, she spun right into Lady Catterly.

The cat's headdress wobbled.

"Watch it, you woolly galumph!"
hissed Lady Catterly. "These are
rare dodo feathers!"

"It was an accident," muttered Audrey.
"No need to be catty."

As soon as Lady Catterly had gone,
Scruff turned to Audrey. "Don't worry,"
he said. "She's always like that."

"Shh!" said Jasper, as an enchanting
melody drifted out from the
audition room.

"A diva with all my might…"

The voice was as smooth as silk.

"I didn't know Lady Catterly could
sing!" gasped Scruff.

"Neither did I," said Jasper.

There was the sound of applause.

"Holy moly… She's a tough act to
follow!" Audrey piped up.
"Wish me luck."

It turned out Audrey didn't need it. She had a huge smile on her face as she cycled out from her audition.

"I got through to the final at the Velvet Theatre!" she cried.

"My time to shine!" said Jasper.

The three judges looked up
as he flounced through the
door into the hall.

"Nice outfit,"
said Marvello,
leaning forwards.
"Well, show us
what you've got."

"Hark! Is that a ship ahead?" began Jasper, pulling a telescope from his pocket. "Three days hence, I, Admiral Everett, will—"

"Bor-ing!" shouted Marvello.
"Next!"

"But... I-I performed this very
speech at the Velvet Theatre!"
stammered Jasper.

"Would you like to start again?" said Alvis.

"Yes, please do—" began Bunny.

"Your acting days are over!"
sneered Marvello.

Jasper flung open the door and Scruff bounded over. "How did it go?" he asked. But his friend was already stomping off.

"Who's next?" called the gazelle.

Scruff gulped. Pushing his top hat out of his eyes, he stepped into the audition room.

A little while later, Scruff bounced into the apartment, tail wagging. "I'm in the final!" he yipped. "Jasper?"

He found his friend sulking inside the fort.

"There you are! Marvello said my magic box was shabby but he liked my tricks!"

"Congratulations," Jasper said through gritted teeth.

Scruff flopped down on a cushion.
"I'm sorry you didn't get in," he said.
"But why don't you be my assistant?
It'll be much more fun together!"

"Assistant? Pah!" huffed Jasper.
"I wanted to do my own act."

"I know a way to cheer you up!" said Scruff.

A few minutes later, he returned with
a milkshake. "Sorry, but I made a bit of
a mess," he admitted.

"Well, I'm sure it tastes nice," said Jasper,
taking a sip. He winced and spat the
drink into his handkerchief. "Bleuch!
Is there salt in this?"

Scruff nodded. "It's salty vanilla –
a new flavour I made up!"

"Let's hope you're better at making magic
than milkshakes!" said Jasper. "I'm sorry for
sulking. Perhaps we *should* team up."

"Yay!" said Scruff, wagging his tail.

Scruff tapped a pack of cards and waved his wand. "For my first trick I'm going to—"

"You should do it like this," interrupted Jasper, snatching the wand.

"Abracadabra, ziggedy zaggedy zoo—"

A stream of cards rushed
out and hit Jasper in the eye.
"Ow!" he yelped.

Scruff giggled.

"It's not as easy as it looks!"

"But I want to perform a trick,"
whined Jasper.

"There is something we can try,"
said Scruff. "And you'll be the star
of the show!"

"Oh, really?" said Jasper,
tweaking his bow tie.

Scruff wheeled a cat-sized box out from his room. "Climb inside!"

"No way!" said Jasper. "It's all dusty. Besides it looks like somebody's already in there!" He prodded a pair of paws sticking out of the bottom.

"Don't worry about those for now," said Scruff, pushing them into the box.

Jasper sighed and climbed in.

"Move up to the top," said Scruff, clicking the lid shut. He pushed a button and the fake cat paws popped back out again.

"It's really squishy in here! I hope—"
Jasper fell silent, as Scruff
pulled out a saw.

"What's THAT?" he yelped.

"Don't worry. It's made out of cardboard," said Scruff. "But I still need you to sound scared. That's where your acting skills come in!"

"I *am* scared!" yowled Jasper, as Scruff began to saw away. "I don't want to get a paper cut!"

"Ta-da!" exclaimed Scruff. He pushed
the two halves of the box apart.

When Scruff pushed the box back
together again, Jasper found that he
was still very much intact.

He stepped out, his legs like jelly.
"Well, that was a heart-stopping magic
act! Let's hope it impresses the judges."

The pair practised late into the night
and all the next morning too.

*Maybe we really do stand a chance of
winning,* thought Jasper, as they pushed
the cat-sized box up to the theatre.

Together they wheeled the heavy box
down a long corridor. They stopped to
catch their breath outside a door
guarded by two huge gorillas.

Just as Jasper and Scruff set off
again, the door swung open and
Lady Catterly stepped out.

WHAM!

"Careful!" she hissed, as the box
crashed right into her.

"Oh, I'm sorry," said Scruff.

"You will be," snickered Reginald, peering round the door.

"Ha, ha, good one!" said Oswald, joining him. "Now scram!"

As Jasper and Scruff hurried into their dressing room, they could still hear the sound of the cats' laughter echoing behind them.

They found a mirror and started
to get ready.

"I think the Sophisticats are up
to something," whispered Scruff.
"We'd better keep an eye
on them."

"I'm not sure we can," sighed
Jasper. "Lady Catterly has her
own private dressing room."

"Will the first contestant go to the stage door!" announced the gazelle. "The show is about to begin."

"That's me!" said Audrey.

"I'm sure you'll be brilliant!" said Scruff. "I wish we could watch."

"Scruff, you've given me an idea," said Jasper, as Audrey cycled off.

Jasper and Scruff
peered out
from the wings,
keeping an eye
out for anything
suspicious.

"Look! There are
the judges," said
Scruff, pointing
to a table in front
of the stage.
"But where's
Marvello?"

Bunny and Alvis jumped as the
magician appeared between them
in a puff of purple smoke.

Bang!

"Welcome to the final of
Reach Fur the Stars!" he boomed.
"Tonight's lucky winner will get to
perform here for a week with I, Marvello,
the World's Most Famous Magician.
Now for our first act!"

A spotlight fell on Audrey, who was perched on a high platform. A tightrope stretched from one side of the stage to the other. Underneath was a giant cream pie.

"If this goes wrong, things are bound to get messy," whispered Jasper.

"Oh, I can't look!" said Scruff. He covered his eyes as Audrey set out across the tightrope.

"That was amazing!" he said, peeping between his paws as she reached the other side.

Audrey picked up some juggling clubs and balls, and edged back out on to the tightrope.

Scruff elbowed Jasper as she began to sway from side to side. "Something doesn't look quite right with the rope."

"It's coming loose!" gasped Jasper.

"Audrey!" cried Scruff. But it was too late.

"Whoa!" Audrey began to wobble. She dropped the clubs and tumbled into the giant pie.

Splat!

"Such a good start," said Bunny, dabbing her dress.

"An ambitious act. Maybe too ambitious," said Alvis, combing cream out of his quiff.

"Ugh!" yowled Marvello. "My top hat is ruined! Next!"

Disco music began to play. Milly
and Milo whizzed on to the stage,
swaying in time to the beat.

"At least they've got their feet on the
ground," whispered Jasper.

As the tune grew faster, Milly zipped up a ramp and shot through the air.

Milo got ready to catch her. But just as their paws met, he slipped.

Milly went flying towards the judges' table...

...landing right in Marvello's lap.

"Get off me!" screeched the
magician. "There are track marks
all over my cape."

"Scruff! Do you see that?" said Jasper,
pointing at a pool of something black
and shiny in the middle of the stage.

Before Scruff got a chance to look,
the spotlight moved on to
the judges.

"You just need a
bit more practice,"
said Bunny.

"Um, good effort,"
said Alvis.

"I've certainly never
seen anything like
THAT before,"
said Marvello.

"Next!"

"We're up," said Scruff,
straightening his top hat.

"Something fishy IS going on," said
Jasper. "Keep your eyes peeled."

"For my first trick," announced Scruff.
"I'm going to saw my assistant in half."

Jasper gave a deep bow. He was about to
climb inside the box when Scruff spotted
something hurtling towards them.

"Duck!" shouted Scruff, pushing Jasper out of the way.

Smash!

A large sandbag swung into the box,
dashing it to pieces.

"That's it!" Jasper placed his head in his paws. "We're out of the competition."

"The show's not over yet," said Scruff. "Entertain them with some magic. I'll be back in a jiffy!" He grabbed Audrey's unicycle from the wings and sped off.

Jasper pulled out a deck of cards and tapped them with his wand. This time, he swished it slowly like Scruff had done. The cards danced in the air.

Hmm, thought Jasper. *I don't actually know any more tricks.*

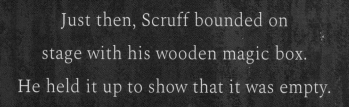

Just then, Scruff bounded on
stage with his wooden magic box.
He held it up to show that it was empty.

"Alakazam!"

He tapped the box with his wand and
a silver tray appeared, with a red-velvet
cake and three milkshakes.

Using their wands, Jasper and Scruff
made the tray float over to the judges.
Then they held paws and took a bow.

"Dazzling!" said
Bunny, taking a sip
of her milkshake.

"Spectacular!" said
Alvis, nibbling on
a cherry.

"Thah wash OK
ashually," said
Marvello through
a mouthful of cake.

Jasper and Scruff skipped off stage,
grinning from ear to ear.

It was time for the final act.

The pair watched from the wings as

the lights dimmed and Lady Catterly

was lowered from the ceiling

on a crescent moon.

"Let's see if any accidents happen during *her* performance," muttered Jasper.

Lady Catterly shimmied to the front of the stage and picked up the microphone.

"Ain't no rival good enough,
Ain't no talent big enough,
Ain't no tricks dirty enough,
To keep me from that trophy!"

As she finished, the judges leaped to their feet to give her a standing ovation.

It was time for the winner to be announced. The contestants gathered on stage.

"It's been an, ahem ... interesting final," said Bunny. "Everyone put on a great show but the w—"

"The winner is Lady Catterly," interrupted Marvello. "Can we all go home now? I need to change my costume."

"As I was saying..." Bunny went on. "The winner is Lady Catterly. She will be performing here from tomorrow night."

"Better luck next time, darlings," trilled Lady Catterly, pushing past Jasper and Scruff to collect her trophy.

"It's no surprise that I won," she gloated. "The theatre is very lucky to have me. I'm sure it will be a sell-out show…"

"The Sophisticats were behind those mishaps, I just know it," said Jasper, as Lady Catterly droned on.

"Well, everyone's going to be here for a while," said Scruff. "Let's investigate."

"Good thing we discovered these air vents on our treasure hunt!" said Scruff, as they climbed inside.

They crawled along until they reached Lady Catterly's dressing room. Peering through a metal grill, they spotted a box of tools.

"Oswald and Reginald must have used that spanner to loosen Audrey's tightrope," said Scruff.

"And look, a bottle of oil," said Jasper. "That's what made Milo slip and fall."

"Shh!" said Scruff. "Someone's coming!"

Lady Catterly sat down at her dressing table and removed her headdress. Jasper and Scruff couldn't believe their eyes. Sitting between her ears was Ruby!

"Oh, thank goodness," said Ruby, hopping on to the dressing table and spreading her wings. "It was very dark under there."

"Just one more week of this," said Lady Catterly. "When I— I mean, WE get a record deal, we can share the profits and your wonderful voice will be heard all around the world."

"It was Ruby who was singing all along!" gasped Scruff. "We should tell the judges!"

"I have a better plan," replied Jasper. "Let's head over to the salon."

"OK," said Scruff. "As long as you don't make me get another shampoo!"

The next evening there was a huge
queue outside the Velvet Theatre.

Disguised as stagehands, Jasper and
Scruff snuck in through the backstage
door and waited in the wings.

The lights dimmed and Lady Catterly
was lowered from the ceiling on the
crescent moon.

"Oooooh!"

gasped the crowd.

As the moon
drifted back up,
Marvello floated
through the air.
He hovered above
Lady Catterly,
performing a card
trick as she sang.

"Ready?" whispered Jasper.

Together Jasper and Scruff pulled
a lever. The moon started to lower,
hooking on to Lady Catterly's curls.

As they pushed the lever, the moon
rose again ... taking her wig with it!

Blushing, Ruby flew up and perched
on the moon. Alone in the spotlight,
Lady Catterly continued to mouth
the words to her song but
no sound came out.

"Boo!"

went the audience.

Lady Catterly looked around in confusion and spotted Ruby. "You've ruined my performance!" she yowled.

"*Your* performance!" cried Marvello. "You're nothing but a fluffy-tailed fraud!"

Lady Catterly picked up the microphone stand and gave Marvello a big whack. Then she stormed off the stage.

The magician swung in the air. "Get me down!" he cried, as the wire holding him caught on the moon. "I am Marvello the Magnificent!"

"Show's over, I guess," said Scruff.

"Not yet," said Jasper. "The show must go on!"

Ruby performed for the rest of the evening to thunderous applause.

"Encore!" shouted the crowd, as she finished her final song.

"OK. Just one more," said Ruby. "But I'd like to invite my friends Jasper and Scruff to join me on stage."

Jasper straightened his bow tie and turned to Scruff. "It is much more fun when we work together."

"Yes, we make a magical double act," agreed Scruff. "Now pass me my saw!"